The DISCARDED Nose Knows

Mmm... apple pie!
Awesome!

by Ellen Weiss
illustrated by Margeaux Lucas

The Kane Press
New York

Acknowledgement: Our thanks to Dr. Jeffrey Cohlberg, Professor of Biochemistry, California State University, Long Beach, for helping to make this book as accurate as possible.

Library of Congress Cataloging-in-Publication Data

Weiss, Ellen, 1949-
        The nose knows / by Ellen Weiss; Illustrated by Margeaux Lucas.
                p. cm. — (Science solves it!)
Summary: A boy with an amazing sense of smell becomes the "Family Nose" when his parents and siblings all come down with colds and cannot smell disgusting and dangerous odors around the house.
  ISBN-10: 1-57565-120-3 (alk. paper)
  ISBN-13: 978-57565-120-0 (alk. paper)
   [1. Smell—Fiction. 2. Nose—Fiction. 3. Odors—Fiction. 4. Cold (Disease)—Fiction. 5. Sick—Fiction. 6. Family life—Fiction.]
I. Lucas, Margeaux, ill. II. Title. III. Series.
   PZ7.W4472 Nq 2002
   [E]—dc21

2002000437

10 9 8 7 6 5 4

First published in the United States of America in 2003 by Kane Press, Inc.
Printed in Hong Kong.

Science Solves It! is a registered trademark of Kane Press, Inc.

Book Design/Art Direction: Edward Miller

www.kanepress.com

Peter was just like any other kid—except for one thing. He had an amazing sense of smell.

Peter could smell cookies baking at the Yum-T-Tum Bakery from two blocks away.

He could smell the difference between chicken noodle soup and turkey noodle soup.

Mmm...turkey!

He could smell a banana in a closed lunch box from across the room.

HOW WE SMELL

1. Cookie smell goes up nose.

2. Cookie smell sticks here.

3. Your brain tells you, "That's a chocolate chip cookie!"

One rainy week in April, everybody in Peter's family had a cold—except Peter.

"I feel awful," said his sister, Tanya, sipping some orange juice.

"Yech!" Peter cried. "Don't drink the juice! It's bad. Can't you taste it?"

"My dose is stuffed," she said.
"What?" he asked.
"My DOSE!" Tanya pointed to her nose.
"I can't smell the juice, so I can't taste it."
"Oh," said Peter. "No wonder."

Did you know?

The wet sticky stuff in your nose is called MUCUS (MEW-cus). When you have a cold, extra mucus stops up your nose and keeps smells from getting to your brain.

At dinner, everybody was sneezing and coughing and blowing their noses—everybody except Peter.

"How come we all have colds, and you don't?" asked Ben.

"I'm lucky," said Peter. "Besides, somebody has to be able to smell around here."

"Will you be the Family Nose until we get better?" asked Mom.

"Sure," said Peter. "Smudge will help me out. He's got a great nose."

After dinner, Peter started his homework.
But he couldn't keep his mind on it. Something
smelled bad—*really* bad.

He followed his nose to Ben's room.

Then he followed his nose to Ben's closet. The
smell got stronger. He opened the closet door.

. . . Aggghh!

Something was on the floor, wrapped in a napkin. "Broccoli!" he gasped. It was gray and slimy, and really, really, REALLY stinky.

"Only one person would hide broccoli in his closet," thought Peter. "My little broccoli-hating brother . . ."

"Uh-oh," said Ben. "You found it."

"Ben," Peter said, "you can't hide broccoli because you don't want to eat it."

"Why not?" asked Ben.

"Because it rots," Peter said. "And then it smells awful."

"I don't smell anything," said Ben.

"YOU have a cold," said Peter.

The next morning Peter's nose woke up
before the rest of him. He smelled coffee,
blueberry pancakes, and. . . ROTTEN EGGS!
He jumped out of bed. Smudge jumped out, too.

"Mom! Dad!" called Peter. "What are you cooking? It smells like rotten eggs."

"GAS!" cried his parents. They rushed into the kitchen and opened the windows.

"Don't come in!" Dad yelled to Peter. "Gas is dangerous." He turned off the stove.

"The pilot light in the stove must have blown out," Mom said after everybody had calmed down. "We didn't notice, because we couldn't smell the gas."

"Good thing we have the Family Nose!" said Dad.

After breakfast Peter went looking for Smudge. "Hey, boy! Want to play ball?"

Smudge didn't jump or wag his tail. He was busy sniffing the air.

"What is it, boy?" asked Peter.

Did you know?

A dog's sense of smell is up to 1,000 times better than ours.

He followed Smudge into the living room. *Phew!* He smelled it—a horrible, swampy odor coming from a flower vase . . .

The water in the vase was green and slimy. The flower stems had rotted, and nobody had noticed.

The Family Nose threw the yucky mess out and washed the vase.

Just as Peter finished, Ben and Tanya ran into the kitchen. "Ben took my Space Monkey T-shirt!" Tanya shouted.

"It's *my* Space Monkey T-shirt!" Ben yelled.

"Maybe I can settle this," Peter said. He sniffed. "This shirt belongs to whoever kept bubble gum in the pocket."

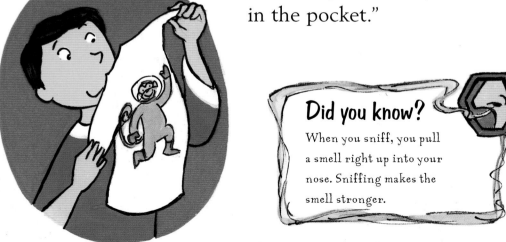

Did you know?

When you sniff, you pull a smell right up into your nose. Sniffing makes the smell stronger.

18

Tanya cheered. Ben moaned.

"You know, Ben," Peter said, "I think I saw a Space Monkey T-shirt on the floor of your closet."

"Really?" said Ben. He was gone in a flash.

"Family Nose!" called Peter's mother from the living room. He found his parents on the couch, exhausted.

"You guys look really tired," Peter said.

"We are," said his mom. "We've been cleaning the house. Grandma and Grandpa are coming over."

"I'll finish," Peter said. "You take a break."

Peter cleaned the bathrooms with pine soap. He polished the furniture with lemon oil. And he scrubbed the kitchen sink with baking soda.

Did you know?

Most people can tell the difference between more than 10,000 smells! But some people have no sense of smell at all!

Then Peter shampooed Smudge with No Stink Shampoo.

When he was finished, Peter took a deep breath. "Everything is clean now," he said. "Even you, Smudge."

Just then the doorbell rang. It was Grandma and Grandpa. They gave Peter a big hug.

"What's in the pot?" Peter asked.

"My special chicken soup," said Grandma.

"The best cold medicine in the world," said Grandpa.

The wonderful smell of Grandma's soup filled the kitchen. "What makes your soup so good, Grandma?" asked Peter.

"Lots of parsley, onions, garlic, celery, and carrots," Grandma said.

"Don't forget the chicken!" added Grandpa.

Peter's mouth was watering. "I can't wait for dinner."

"You don't have to," said Grandma. "Soup's on!"

"Hey!" Tanya said. "I can taste the onions!
I must be getting better!"

"Grandma's done it again," said Grandpa.

"This soup has no taste," said Ben.

"It's *very* tasty," Peter said.
"You can't taste it because
you have a cold."

Did you know?

Your sense of smell helps you taste!
Try this: Hold your nose and sip some
lemonade. What does it taste like?

"Peter didn't catch the cold," Dad told Grandma, "so he's the Family Nose."

"He's saved us from all kinds of terrible things," said Mom. "Gas . . ."

"And sour orange juice," said Tanya.

"And smelly flowers," said Dad.

"And they don't even know about the broccoli!"

After dinner, Peter took Smudge to the park. They met Smudge's best friend and played his favorite game—Frisbee.

"Being the Family Nose is hard work," thought
Peter when he got home. "I'm going right to bed."
Peter took off his right shoe, then his left.
That's when he noticed it. "Yuck!" he said.
"Bubblegum! But why didn't I smell it?"

Just as Peter crawled under the covers, he gave
one loud sneeze. *Aaah. . .aaaaa. . .CHOOO!*
"Peter! Was that you?" called Mom.

The whole family came into Peter's room.
"You caught the family cold!" Tanya said.
Peter nodded. "I can't smell a thing."
"So you're not the Family Nose any more?"
Ben asked.
"That's right," said Peter. "Now I'm the
Family *STUFFED* Nose."

I can observe!

THINK LIKE A SCIENTIST

Peter thinks like a scientist—and so can you!
We learn about the world around us by using our five
senses. We see, hear, smell, taste, and touch. Scientists
call this **observing**.

Look Back

In this story Peter used his super sense of smell to observe.
He used other senses too. Which of his five senses is Peter
using on page 16 when he observes Smudge sniffing?
Which senses would Peter use if he observed Smudge
barking? Can you find more places in the story where
Peter used different senses?

Try This!

Be Nose for A Day! Keep a Smell Journal and write
or draw what you smelled. Then draw a picture of how
you looked when you smelled it!

Your Smell Journal
might look like this: